MY PETER RABBIT™ KEEPSAKE

A Photograph Album

Devised and compiled
by Frances Brace

With new reproductions from the original illustrations by
BEATRIX POTTER™
F. WARNE & Co

Beatrix Potter, whose familiar characters decorate these pages,
was a keen photographer, and her father Rupert Potter was so expert
that he used to take photographs for use as reference by famous
painters of his day. He took this picture of Beatrix and
her brother Bertram when Beatrix was twelve.

FREDERICK WARNE

Published by the Penguin Group, 27 Wrights Lane, London W8 5TZ, England
Penguin Books USA Inc., 375 Hudson Street, New York, New York 10014, USA
Penguin Books Australia Ltd, Ringwood, Victoria, Australia
Penguin Books Canada Ltd, 10 Alcorn Avenue, Toronto, Ontario, Canada M4V 3B2
Penguin Books (N.Z.) Ltd, 182-190 Wairau Road, Auckland 10, New Zealand

Penguin Books Ltd, Registered Offices: Harmondsworth, Middlesex, England

First published as *My Photograph Album* 1988 by Frederick Warne
This edition first published 1993
3 5 7 9 10 8 6 4

Text copyright © Frances Brace, 1988, 1993
New reproductions of Beatrix Potter's book illustrations copyright © Frederick Warne & Co., 1987
Original copyright in Beatrix Potter's illustrations © Frederick Warne & Co., 1902, 1903, 1904, 1906,
1907, 1908, 1909, 1910, 1911, 1913, 1917, 1918, 1928

Frederick Warne & Co. is the owner of all rights, copyrights and trademarks
in the Beatrix Potter character names and illustrations.

ISBN 0 7232 4121 X

Typeset by Rowland Phototypesetting (London) Ltd
Printed and bound in Great Britain by William Clowes Limited
Beccles and London

INSTRUCTIONS

Here is your very own photograph album. It gives you the chance to arrange your photographs in the most imaginative and attractive way.

•

Choose a photograph for each page. You may already have a suitable photograph or you may want to take a picture especially for it.

•

Decide what you would like to write about the photograph. You may want to copy some of the suggested words and phrases, but use your own ideas wherever you can.

•

Stick or glue the photograph on the page using a non-solvent-based glue or special mounts. Make sure that the picture hides the list of 'Words you may like to use'. If necessary, trim your picture so that it fits neatly on the page.

•

When you have filled in all the sections you will find three pages at the end of the book where you can put extra photographs and captions on any subject of your choice.

•

If you have an enlarged photograph of yourself, your family or an important occasion, you can complete the album by mounting it here to cover these instructions. It will then form the first page of a book all about you and your own life, which you can keep for yourself or give to a very special friend or relative.

Words you may like to use
my mother
my father
a monkey
a prince
a princess
a frog
a doll

From *The Tale of The Flopsy Bunnies*

My name is Brayden Legend Kravitz

When I was a baby I looked just like Daddy

Daniel A Kravitz

Words you may like to use

blond	blue
brown	brown
black	grey
red	green

smart
pretty
angelic
naughty
sad

My birthday is   April 12 2013

My hair is   Brown/Black   and my eyes are   Gray /blue

Here I am looking

From *The Tale of Timmy Tiptoes*

Here is Benjamin Bunny's family tree:

Benjamin's Grandparents

Mrs Bunny = Old Mr Benjamin (Bouncer) Bunny   Josephine Bunny (Mrs Rabbit) = Mr Rabbit

Benjamin = Flopsy   Mopsy   Cotton-tail = Black Rabbit   Peter

Flopsy Bunny 1   Flopsy Bunny 2   Flopsy Bunny 3   Flopsy Bunny 4   Flopsy Bunny 5   Flopsy Bunny 6

Here is my family tree:

From *The Tale of The Flopsy Bunnies*

· MY FAMILY ·

This is a photograph of ....

From *The Tale of Peter Rabbit*

· MY FAMILY ·

Words you may like to use
brother
step-brother
sister
half-sister
cousin
aunt
uncle

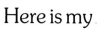

Here is my ....

....

From *The Tale of Peter Rabbit*

· MY FAMILY ·

Words you may like to use

grandmother

granny

grandma

grandfather

grandad

grandpa

godparents

This picture shows . . . .

. . . .

From *The Tale of The Flopsy Bunnies*

From *The Tale of Peter Rabbit*

From *The Tale of Mr. Jeremy Fisher*

From *The Tale of Timmy Tiptoes*

From *The Tale of Johnny Town-Mouse*

· MY HOME ·

My address is 5789 Mission Center Rd #21
San Diego CA 92108

I live in a San Diego Until 2014

Words you may like to use
house
flat
apartment
castle
hotel
bungalow
cottage

· MY FRIENDS ·

Words you may like to use
    at the park
    in the garden
    in the street
    in town
    in the country
    in school

From *The Tale of Mr. Jeremy Fisher*

My friends are called ....

....

We like to spend our time ....

· MY FRIENDS ·

From *The Tale of Johnny Town-Mouse*

What we enjoy most is . . . .

. . . .

. . . .

· GAMES ·

Words you may like to use

catch

tag

football

dressing up

computer games

hide-and-seek

pillow fights

The games I like best are ....

....

From *The Tale of Tom Kitten*

·GAMES·

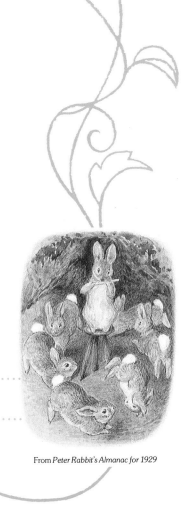

We play . . . .

From Peter Rabbit's Almanac for 1929

From *The Tale of Tom Kitten*

From *The Tale of Benjamin Bunny*

From *Appley Dapply's Nursery Rhymes*

From *The Tale of The Flopsy Bunnies*

· DRESSING UP ·

When I wore this outfit I was ....

....

But I most like wearing ....

·SPECIAL OCCASIONS·

Words you may like to use
Christmas
Ramadan
Hanukkah
Thanksgiving
New Year
wedding
birthday

From *The Tale of Mrs. Tittlemouse*

Here we are celebrating..

·SPECIAL OCCASIONS·

Words you may like to use

decorated the room

prepared the food

danced

sang

laughed

ate and drank

On that day we ....

....

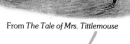

From The Tale of Mrs. Tittlemouse

· MY PARTY ·

At this ....

the guests were ....

....

....

....

....

The games we played were ....

....

....

....

The best party foods are ....

....

From *The Tale of Johnny Town-Mouse*

·MY PARTY·

Words you may like to use

birthday party	sandwiches
tea party	crisps
dinner party	ice-cream
school party	cake
picnic	chips

•

musical chairs
pass the parcel
hunt the thimble

From *The Tale of Johnny Town-Mouse*

Words you may like to use
- the lake
- the sea
- the country
- the park
- the mountains
- the zoo
- the museum

From *The Tale of Mr. Jeremy Fisher*

On...

we went to...

·OUR DAY OUT·

Words you may like to use
playing
looking at things
collecting
having a picnic
getting wet
fishing
walking

We spent the day ....

....

From *The Tale of Mr. Jeremy Fisher*

· OUR HOLIDAY ·

This is what we did

....

....

From *The Tale of Pigling Bland*

· OUR HOLIDAY ·

Words you may like to use

vacation	stayed up late
boat	visited interesting
plane	places
train	adventure
bus	climbing
tent	exploring
hotel	swimming
farmhouse	beach

From *The Tale of Johnny Town-Mouse*

·WATER·

This photograph shows ....

....

....

From *The Tale of Tom Kitten*

· ACTION ·

Words you may like to use

me dancing

us running

skipping

hopping

swinging

walking

crawling

Here you can see ....

....

....

From *The Tale of Jemima Puddle-Duck*

·TRAVEL·

Words you may like to use

bus
car
boat
bike
skis
skateboard
roller skates
plane
train

From *The Tale of Squirrel Nutkin*

I like to travel by . . . .

· ANIMALS ·

The animal I like best is ....

What I like about it is ....

....

From The Tale of Mrs. Tiggy-Winkle

From *The Tale of Peter Rabbit*

From *The Tale of Jemima Puddle-Duck*

From *The Tailor of Gloucester*